KV-191-130

To Graiglwyd 1974-2006

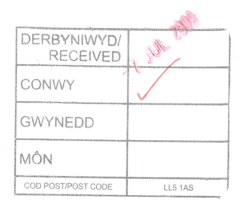

DERBYNIWYD/ RECEIVED	
CONWY	✓
GWYNEDD	
MÔN	
COD POST/POST CODE	LL5 1AS

Anglesey, Conwy & Gwynedd Library Services

GW 6000747 8

HJ	
	£5.99

Published in 2008 by Pont Books, an imprint of
Gomer Press, Llandysul, Ceredigion SA44 4JL

ISBN 978 1 84323 812 6

A CIP record for this title is available from the British Library.

© Jac Jones, 2008

Jac Jones has asserted his moral rights under the
Copyright, Designs and Patents Act, 1988 to be identified
as author and illustrator of this work.

All rights reserved. No part of this book may be reproduced,
stored in a retrieval system, or transmitted in any form or by any means,
electronic, electrostatic, magnetic tape, mechanical, photocopying, recording
or otherwise without permission in writing from the above publishers.

This book is published with the financial support of the
Welsh Books Council.

Printed and bound in Wales at
Gomer Press, Llandysul, Ceredigion

GW 6000747 8

Move*Over, Rover

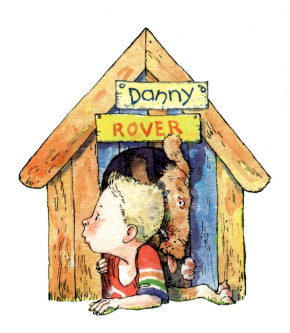

JAC JONES

Pont

Danny lived with Mam and Dad and Sara
in a village in the middle of Wales.

Rover lived there too, in a little house all of his own.

Rover's idea of fun was find-and-fetch.

He liked to dig huge holes ... and hide in them.

He loved to scare and scatter cats.

He thought messing about in mud was marvellous.

Whatever he did, Rover got a pat on the head.

'That's not fair!' said Danny. 'I'd like a pat on the head too.' He thought for a long, long time. 'Move over, Rover,' he said.

'Are you a doggy, Danny?' asked Mr Norman
next door.

'Bow wow!' barked Danny.

'Danny, stop digging up my daisies!' scolded Mam.
'Grrr!' growled Danny, the dangerous dog.

'Stop snapping at that Siamese!' shouted Sara as Danny raced round and round the rhubarb.

'That's enough find-and-fetch,' said Dad. 'I'm fed up'.

'Move over, Rover', said Danny. 'I've been a dog
all day and I haven't been patted once.'

Rover looked at Danny and raced out of the kennel, barking at him to follow.

Danny barked back and bounded after him.

The doggy mates had a mad and mucky mud bath.

Mam, Dad and Sara just couldn't stop laughing.

Mam wiped the mud off Danny's nose
and gave him a kiss.

Dad patted him on the head.
'Who's a mucky pup then?' he laughed.

Danny was so happy.
He wished he had a tail to wag!

Other picture books by Jac Jones

Ble Mae Pawb?

Rhiannon Rowlands

CYFRES BYD LLIWGAR MABON A MABLI

Taid ar Binnau

Meinir Pierce Jones

CYFRES BYD LLIWGAR MABON A MABLI

Alison and the bully monsters

Jac Jones

Druan o M...

Brenda Wyn Jones

CYFRES BYD LLIWGAR MABON A MABLI

Mymryn O Dric!

Meinir Pierce Jones

CYFRES BYD LLIWGAR MABON A MABLI

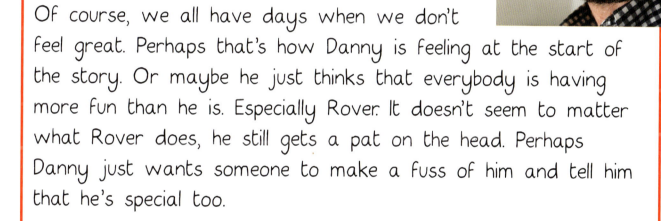

Hi

When I thought about making this story,
I wanted it to be a happy book. I wanted to
make you smile, even if you weren't smiling
when you took it down from the shelf.

Of course, we all have days when we don't
feel great. Perhaps that's how Danny is feeling at the start of
the story. Or maybe he just thinks that everybody is having
more fun than he is. Especially Rover. It doesn't seem to matter
what Rover does, he still gets a pat on the head. Perhaps
Danny just wants someone to make a fuss of him and tell him
that he's special too.

That's why Rover and I wanted you to have something special
for yourself. Over the page you will find something to remind
your family and friends that we all deserve a pat – even when
we're in the dog house!

Jac

All About ME

My name is _____

I live at _____

My best friend is _____

I am good at _____

I like it when _____

The best thing about me is _____

Certificate

This is to certify that

_____

deserves

a pat on the head
just for being

_____

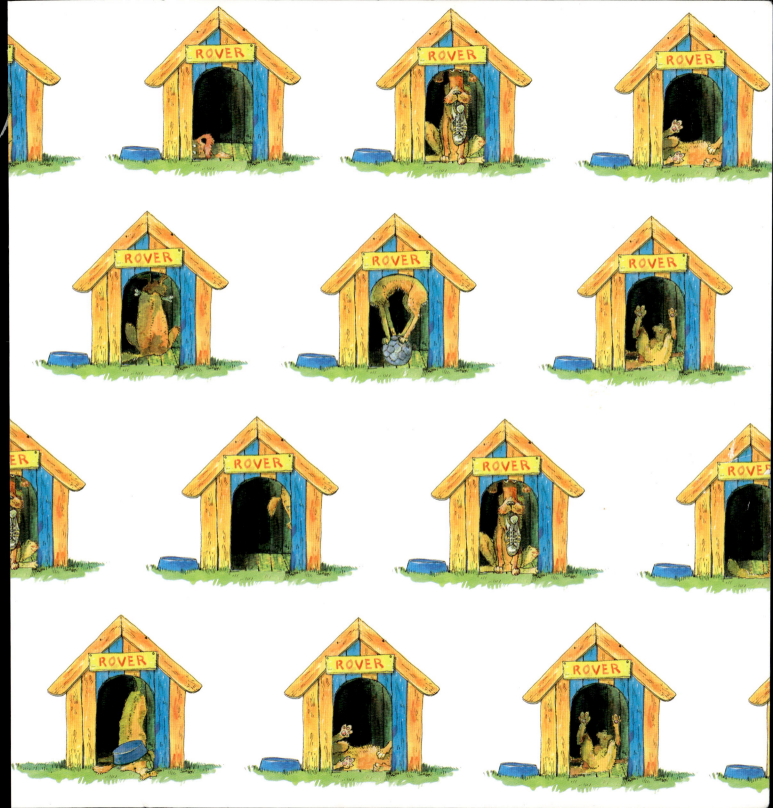